Simon and the Witch in School

Margaret Stuart Barry

Illustrated by Linda Birch

Young Lions

First published in Great Britain 1987
by William Collins Sons & Co. Ltd
First published in Young Lions 1988

Young Lions is an imprint of
the Children's Division, part of
the Collins Publishing Group,
8 Grafton Street, London W1X 3LA

Printed and bound in Great Britain by
William Collins Sons & Co. Ltd, Glasgow

Simon and the Witch in School

Simon's friend the witch discovers she can no longer understand her Spell Book. When she tries to magic up a teapot she keeps getting cabbages, or footballs, or pudding basins.

"You'll just have to come to school and learn to read again," said Simon.

Having the witch in the classroom livens things up enormously! She's hopeless at maths, hopeless at spelling, hopeless at PE, but excellent at thinking up ideas, especially if she's stolen them from someone else. She manages to come top in the exams by cheating madly, and her performance as the Wicked Fairy in the school production of *The Sleeping Beauty* steals the show. It's doubtful if she learns anything; she's too busy causing chaos.

This, the sixth book about the adventures of Simon and the witch, is a special publication to tie in with the BBC TV series.

Also available in Young Lions

Contents

For my daughter, Jane

The Battered Spell Book

IT WAS the first day of the Christmas term. Simon was eating his breakfast very slowly and his mother was trying to make him hurry.

"It will be Christmas in no time at all," she was telling him for the umpteenth time.

Simon grunted.

"Can I go round and see the witch on the way home?" he asked. "It's ages since I've seen her."

"All right," agreed his mother, "but how many times have I told you not to call that unfortunate old woman a witch?"

The witch was Simon's best friend and he knew she was a witch. She'd done so many amazing things, he was always surprised that other people could not believe she was a real witch. His school friend, Jimmy Watson, believed of course, but that was about it. Jimmy was slumped against the hall radiator, looking tragic. His small body was all boarded up in a new shirt and stiff trousers. He was looking desperate.

"Isn't first day back hideous?" he greeted Simon. "I wish I was an old man, just sitting on a bench, or just sitting in a cafe, or just . . ."

"You're so silly, Jimmy Watson," scoffed Sally, who was the class swot-pot and knew everything. "Learning new things is really exciting."

Jimmy muttered that it would be really exciting if Sally could learn to keep her mouth shut. He was just wishing he hadn't said it, as Sally started towards him, when Mr Bodley, the headmaster, appeared.

That was the start of the new term. The children were sitting in rows, already dozing off; Mr Bodley was booming and roaring the way he always did, and Miss Phoeble, the class teacher, was perched on the edge of the stage like a rather seedy bird.

Meanwhile, the witch was having a sleep-in. She wasn't actually properly sleeping, but was lying on her back counting spiders on her bedroom ceiling. If she attacked quickly, she reckoned, she'd be able to catch fifteen of them and then she could have them on toast for breakfast. Without warning, she shot out of bed and caught all fifteen spiders in her hairnet.

"Gottum!" she cackled, "but I wish they'd sell spiders in the supermarket. I'm getting too old to keep jumping up at the ceiling and me bed's getting ruined as well."

She munched up the spiders on toast and swilled

them down with a mug of sarsaparilla.

George, the witch's cat, had been out hunting all night. He prowled in, cold and irritable. His black fur was matted together with mud, soot, dead leaves, even deader bits of mouse and drain water. He didn't smell very friendly. Nor did he feel it. He limped dramatically over to his bowl and sniffed. It contained a toast crumb and a single spider's leg. How was that supposed to keep his body and soul together? He threw the witch a nasty, dirty look, but she was busy, so he contented himself with eating the leg of the television. It wasn't his favourite sort of wood, but he'd already eaten most of the tastier furniture around. The witch didn't notice George. She was grumbling on about her spell book. It was all battered and muddled and she was getting in a niggly wiggly mood as she tried to make it out.

"B . . A . . T spells PUDDING! Somebody has been tampering with the pages! Somebody has been eating letters and words willy nilly! It must have been that rat-bag of a cat, that monstrous thieving walking doormat with whiskers!"

George looked huffy. It was bad enough having to keep himself alive eating furniture without being accused of things he HADN'T done. He decided he'd jolly well run away. He squidged under the door and disappeared.

"And STOP out!" the witch screeched after him. She was trying to magic up a teapot and kept getting a cabbage. It was becoming very boring.

So was school, Simon thought. It was still Assembly, and Mr Bodley was rumbling on about old people. He was chunnering about a project to raise money to help the aged.

"We've got to be kind to old people," he bellowed, completely waking Jimmy up. "Some children are very mean to old people. They think, that just because people are old, they're deaf, dumb, and daft as well! They insult old people and play sly tricks on them and poke fun at them."

"Why's he getting so cross?" whispered Jimmy.

"Dunno," whispered Simon back. "I think he's feeling old himself or something."

Mr Bodley gave Simon a terrifying look, but hastily finished by saying that they were going to spend the term collecting money for the old, and that the mayor was going to give a prize for the best fund raising idea.

"Big deal!" thought the children as they trudged back to class.

At long last, it was time to go home, and Simon ran all the way to the witch's house.

"Come in!" yelled the witch, in a muffled voice.

Simon looked around expectantly but couldn't see her. The witch's sitting room was ten times more untidy than usual. The table was piled up with cabbages, pumpkins, footballs, pudding basins, and cuddly toys. Underneath the table was an assortment of stuffed snakes, fluffy parrots, a donkey with one ear and no tail, and mountains of bags of popcorn. Also under the table was the witch, lying in a cock-eyed heap and half stuck under the donkey with one ear and no tail.

"What on earth are you doing!" exclaimed Simon.

"What does it look as if I'm doing?" the witch snapped. "I'm *trying* to make a teapot and keep getting all this rubbish!"

She heaved the donkey out of the way and struggled up, hot and bothered. "You see this blooming book here," she threw a handful of pump-

kins and pudding basins onto the floor, "it says, b . . a
. . t spells pudding. It never used to! And it says, p . . o
. . t spells cabbage. And it says, t . . e . . a . . p . . o . . t
spells stuffed snake, and that can't be right either!"
Simon could see at once that the witch's spell book
had huge teeth marks in it, and filthy paw marks, and
distinct cat-mouth shaped lumps missing out of it,
which explained why nothing was making sense. But
he grinned and said, "You can't spell! You've
forgotten how to read that's all."

"I haven't forgotten how to read!" screeched the
witch, uncertainly.

"Then why have you got a room full of rubbish,
when all you wanted was a teapot?"

"They're all *useful* things," sulked the witch.

"But you can't make a cup of tea in them," laughed Simon. "You'll just have to come to school and learn how to read again."

"SCHOOL!" screamed the witch. "I hate that place."

She magicked her face bright green and looked at Simon, slyly.

"I'll call for you in the morning," Simon said.

There was a spot on the end of the witch's nose, and she made it turn orange and flash on and off like a traffic light.

"You will be ready, won't you?" Simon added. "And you'll have to make yourself look tidy," he said, pretending he hadn't noticed a single thing wrong with the witch's appearance.

"But I'm shaking like a jelly," complained the witch, wobbling herself as hard as she could. "See!"

She looked up between wobbles, but Simon had gone.

"That poor old woman," said Simon's mother. "You should have left her in peace. And what on earth is Mr Bodley going to say?"

"I don't know," said Simon. Out of his mother's hearing, he added, "but I think he'll be quite mad!"

The New Girl

THE WITCH was feeling extremely cosy. Her duvet was like a warm boat and she was floating around the Bay of Biscay. She had just marmalised ten thousand pirates, taken all their gold off them, and bounty, whatever that was, and was going to travel overland to drop in unexpectedly on her sister, Tombola, when her alarm clock went off.

"Xmas!" exclaimed the witch.

She leapt out of bed, still asleep, and went downstairs, switched on Breakfast TV and wondered why the presenter was leaning to one side. Then she noticed that one of the television legs had been half eaten.

"It's a lovely day for doing it," the television was saying.

"For doing *what*?" the witch wondered.

Then she remembered with terrible loathing that it

was a school day.

Did she need to wash her face? No, she didn't because she jolly well wasn't going to school, and she shot back to bed.

Going to sleep again at the wrong time was not easy, and the witch could hear Simon, knocking. Then she could hear him walking about downstairs.

Simon looked up at the ceiling. He could hear ridiculous, pretend snores. "It's twenty to nine," he called, "and your telly's on".

The witch appeared, looking very sulky.

"Do I look all right?" she asked, sheepishly. She was wearing her best coat, the one with the fur collar, which looked like a dead relation of George's. And she was carrying, as usual, her handbag, containing her magic wand, pension book, spare knickers and toothbrush in case she was invited to stay anywhere without warning, and she had made a fairish attempt to sponge the soup stains off her front.

"You look all right," said Simon. "You do know we're late, don't you?" he panted, as they jogged to school the long way round.

"Does it matter?" asked the witch.

Mr Bodley had started Assembly. It was only the second day of the term. The rest of the term stretched before him like the Sahara Desert. All these children sitting in front of him, waiting for him to say something. Nothing out of the ordinary ever hap-

15

pened. He started to sing,
"All things bright and beautiful,
All creatures great and small . . ."
There was a crash as the witch arrived at the back
of the hall . . . "All creatures great and small"? The
witch was interested at once. Where were they? What
were they? Spiders? Beetles? She didn't mind which,

she'd had a quickish breakfast and she was still hungry. Perhaps these creatures great and small were hiding under the radiators, and she flopped down to look.

"Excuse me, my good woman," Mr Bodley began, "but I think you're in the wrong building."

"I know perfectly well where I is," shouted the witch, "and I've come here to be learnt. Worse luck."

"It's that awful old faggot again," whispered Sally.

Several other children began to recognize the witch. They had never expected to see her again and were both delighted and slightly scared, at the same time. Mr Bodley was speechless. He slipped out of the hall to ring the Education Office but the person on the other end of the phone said she couldn't see anywhere in the book of rules where it said witches weren't allowed to go to school, so he came back to Assembly and said he supposed the witch had better go into Simon's class.

"We'll see how you get on," he said.

"Get on what?" the witch asked.

"Lead out!" bellowed Mr Bodley.

The witch bagged herself a desk beside the window.

"Er, we've got a new pupil today," Miss Phoeble began, nervously. "I want you to help her as much as you can and make her feel welcome." The witch gave a toothy grin all round and looked suitably new.

"I'm not going to help her," whispered Sally behind her hand. "She's just a crafty old beggar woman. She's up to no good. Just you wait and see."

The witch shot Sally a malignant look.

"I'll help her, Miss," squeaked Jimmy Watson. "She can borrow my crayons, or anything. And I'll

play with her."

"Creep!" said Sally.

"Will you give out the maths books, Simon, please," interrupted Miss Phoeble, hastily.

The class settled down, glancing occasionally at the witch to see what she would do.

"What's maths?" the witch hissed at Simon.

"Just sums," whispered Simon.

"Somes? — Some what? — Some rhubarb? Some rice pudding? Some battle-ships? Some monkeys up a gum tree?"

"Just look at them and try," answered Simon, mildly exasperated.

The witch opened her book and stared woodenly at it. "S'load of rubbish!" she said to herself. She chewed the end of her pencil and spat out the bits. Suddenly, she got up and looked at Sally's book.

"Go and do your own work, you big cheat!" screeched Sally.

"All right, I will then," snorted the witch. "I'll do my own work because these sums are very boring."

And she wiggled her magic wand at all the books and they instantly changed into helpings of fish and chips.

"What's this?" gasped Miss Phoeble.

"Take-aways," giggled the witch. "I got fed up with adding ups."

The children were amazed and delighted. At

playtime they all crowded round the witch. They wanted to know if she could do any more magic, just to prove that she really was a real witch, and not just a crafty beggar woman, like Sally had said.

"I can do any trick in the world," boasted the witch, "but magic wands get worn out quite quickly, you know, and on my pension I can't afford to keep buying new ones."

"That's right," said Simon, who was shocked how quickly some of the children had forgotten the fish and chips. "And anyway," he added, "she's only come here for a short time until she learns to read, and then she's going again."

The children stared at the witch curiously. How could a grown-up as old as she was not be able to read? Most of them were up to book five. Some of them were on to proper library books. On the other hand, none of them could make books turn into fish and chips.

After playtime they went to the hall for P.E. Miss Phoeble was in a long pair of shorts, demonstrating bunny hops.

"Hop, hop, lightly as you can," she was puffing. The children were not doing too well, except for Sally. They were rolling over sideways in heaps. The witch too was stuck. She was upside down but her feet seemed stuck to the floor. Nor had she the faintest idea where she was because her skirt had fallen over

her head and her nose was wedged inside her
handbag. At that moment, Mr Bodley came in,
accompanied by the mayor who was wearing his gold
chain. Mr Bodley shuddered at the sight of the witch,
and Miss Phoeble hastily tidied herself up.

"Sit, children," she said.

"Now what?" they wondered.

Mr Bodley was on the stage with the mayor.

"That cissy in the gold necklace fancies me," the
witch hissed at Simon.

"Sssh, that's the mayor," Simon said.

The mayor was beaming at the witch.

"Who is that dear old lady?" he asked Mr Bodley.

"Dear old . . .? Oh, that's Mrs . . . she's a new pupil," Mr Bodley told him.

"Fancy!" said the mayor. "Quite charming."

Mr Bodley then told the children that the mayor wanted to hear of any good ideas they might have about raising money for the old people's home.

"And of course there'll be a little prize for the best idea," the mayor chuckled in the jolly sort of voice he kept specially trained for talking to children.

"More scrounging!" Sally snorted on the way home.

"Still," said Jimmy Watson, "it'll be better than lessons. It's bound to waste a nice lot of time."

Simon's mother was setting the table for tea.

"I've got to think of an idea for making money," announced Simon. "What do you think?"

"About what, dear?"

"About making money."

"Why, don't I give you enough pocket money?"

"Nearly," said Simon. "But I mean at school – it's to stop us being mean to old people: helping them instead of making fun of them."

His mother looked puzzled.

"I mean the money's for the old people's home, to get it a hair dryer and a telly and things like that."

"Oh, I see," said Simon's mother. She piled some beans onto Simon's toast. "Jumble sales are the usual. I tell you what, I've got to call round to Horty Hall with some envelopes for Lady Fox-Custard. She's usually the one with the best fund-raising ideas."

"Oh, she is, is she!" exclaimed the witch.

"Did you hear a voice just then?" asked Simon's mother. "It was coming from over by the window."

Simon went to look. He thought he caught a glimpse of the witch's skirts scuttling across the lawn but he couldn't be sure.

"No matter," said his mother, "I'll just give her ladyship a ring while you pop up and change."

"Change what?" groaned Simon.

"Into a nice clean shirt. You can't go round to Horty Hall in your school shirt, can you?"

Simon grumbled to himself as he followed his mother along the road to the hall. Lady Fox- Custard was his worst favourite sort of person. She was a big fat fish face, he decided. She was so stuck up it was difficult for her to see anything lower than her own nose, she never stopped boasting. They were approaching the gates and the two plaster lions on the gate posts looked down on them haughtily, or would have done if they'd had fewer vulgar looking pigeons sitting on them.

A very clean young man bowed Simon and his mother in.

"That's my new man, Hopkins," cooed Lady Fox-Custard, "but I call him Poppet because that's just what he is. *So* well trained." Poppet walked stiffly out of the door, but he gave Simon a secret sort of wink as he passed him.

Lady Fox-Custard was wearing a huge, flowered dress and was pouring tea. Next to the tea things, balanced on a little table, was a large vase.

"I believe we're to have a fund-raising competition at the school with a prize for the best idea?"

"So Simon tells me?" said Simon's mother. "I think jumble sales are the quickest way of raising money. Not very interesting perhaps, but at least everyone comes."

"Mm," said Lady Fox-Custard, absently. "Would you like a napkin, dear?" she said, pointedly, as Simon tried to free his fingers from a chocolate eclair. "I can see you are looking at my lovely pot." (Simon hadn't in fact noticed it at all.) "It's Crown Derby, in case you didn't know, and I expect you didn't. *Dreadfully* expensive."

Simon struggled without success to look interested. There was never any end to Lady Fox-Custard's bragging. He wondered why his mother didn't seem to notice. She was too nice, that was probably why.

"Yes, I do love gorgeous things about me," Lady Fox-Custard went on. "How are you getting on at school?" she asked, suddenly.

"All right," mumbled Simon. It was the stickiest eclair he had ever done battle with.

"I've got a nephew called Cuthbert and he's dreadfully clever. He wants to work at the Home Office."

"Really?" said Simon's mother. "How old is he?"

"Seven," said Lady Fox-Custard. "As a matter of fact, Simon, you'll be meeting him in school. You could be his little friend."

"Mm," mumbled Simon, horrified.

As soon as Simon and his mother had left, Lady Fox-Custard rang for Poppet. "Quick quick, pass me the phone will you?"

The phone was only a metre away from where she was sitting, but she had hired Poppet from Rent-a-Butler at some cost and believed in getting her money's worth. "Never buy a dog and bark yourself" her great-grandfather, Lord Ian-Idle had been fond of telling her.

"Your phone, madam," said Poppet, who had been taught that a duchess and a pig were the same if they were paying.

"Mr Bodley? . . . ah, Headmaster — I've just had the greatest idea for your little fund-raising competition — a *Jumble* sale! And I am willing to allow it to be held right here in Horty Hall!"

"Oh, wonderful!" said Mr Bodley, bowing over the phone.

Lady Fox-Custard smiled smugly and rang the bell for Poppet, telling him he could replace the phone. For one fleeting moment, she thought she saw a hideous nose and two terrible eyes at the window, but of course it must have been her imagination. But then she heard a scrunch.

It was the sort of scrunch begonias make when they are being trampled on. Lady Fox-Custard shot to the window.

The witch knew that she was about to be discovered. "Here, pussy, pussy," she said.

"What on earth do you think you are doing?"

shrieked Lady Fox-Custard.

"Doing?" said the witch, looking up with pretence startlement. "Oh . . . *Doing*! I'm looking for my cat. His name is George. He's black and not awfully well looking. I fear for his health actually. You haven't seen him prowling around these parts have you?"

"No, I have NOT!" yelled Lady Fox-Custard. "But I *have* seen what you've just done to me prize begonias. They're ruined!"

The witch looked down at her feet which were sticky with the sap of snapped begonia stems.

"Oh golly! Are they begonias?" she gasped. "I thought they was titchy rhubarb leaves. I've got rhubarb all over my garden. It's like a weed, isn't it? You can't get rid of it. I keep chopping mine down and digging it up, but you can't kill it. Begonias eh! That's a new one on me."

"Get out!" screeched Lady Fox-Custard.

"So sorry," said the witch, escaping craftily.

George was still missing when she arrived home. It was not like him to stay away so long. He was obviously sulking about something. Probably because she forgot to feed him now and again.

"Oh well, to hec with him. *Stay* lost!" she snorted at the empty hearthrug. She sat down at the table, licked her pencil, and started to write a note, painfully slowly.

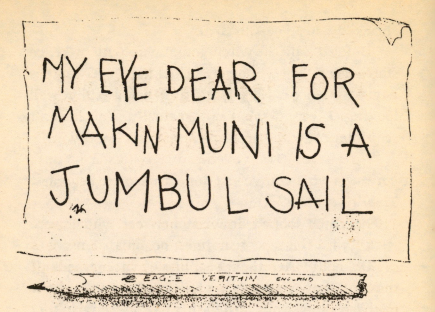

MY EYE DEAR FOR MAKIN MUNI IS A JUMBUL SAIL

Cackling gleefully, she stuffed the note into her handbag and went to bed. She kept wondering what the prize would be. It was bound to be something pretty good. She would have to go up on the stage and everybody would clap her. Fox-Custard would be livid! Serves her right for pinching other people's ideas!

The Smashing Giraffe

THE CHILDREN had arrived fairly early, for once.

"Just wait till you hear about *my* idea," Sally was saying. "I had a word with Mr Bodley last night about seating arrangements in the hall, and about microphones."

"What do you want seating rangemunts for?" asked Sharon Dupont.

"Ah," said Sally, tapping her nose. "I'm not telling anyone yet. Good ideas get stolen. There are people who think nothing of eavesdropping."

The witch, who had had her ear pressed too hard to the door, fell in, all of a heap, and rolled across the classroom like a skittle.

"Whoops!" she said. "Some fool's been polishing the floors."

"Were you listening?" accused Sally.

"What? About seating arrangements? Certainly not. I've got my *own* idea – it's in the bag," she grinned, tapping her handbag and looking terribly cheerful. "I am, you might say, quietly confident."

"Ridiculous old hag!" muttered Sallly.

"You'll never *guess* what I've thought of!" Jimmy was saying. "I've said that our house could be turned into a sweet factory and my mum could make millions of gob-stoppers, cheap."

"They'd be useful," scoffed Sally.

"I thought we would make little sachets of lavender," said Sharon Dupont.

Everybody completely ignored this idea.

Miss Phoeble arrived and said, "Mr Bodley wants all your ideas *now* to give to the mayor for judging. But they *must* be in writing, that's obligatory."

"I've wrote mine," said the witch, sitting with her arms folded across her bosom, her feet together, and an obedient expression on her normally wicked face.

"I can *tell* you now," said Sally. "My idea was to have a huge quiz in the hall, like University Challenge."

"Uck!" cried Jimmy Watson, grabbing hold of his throat to stop himself from being sick. "I'll stay off school with mumps if *that* idea wins."

But a lot of people were impressed with Jimmy Watson's own idea.

Meanwhile, the mayor was sitting in his town hall wearing his gold chain and cocked hat, and wondering if it was nearly lunchtime. That boring, booming headmaster, had given him all these boring, blooming fund-raising ideas to sort out. Why couldn't he have judged it himself by just sticking a pin in them?

"Let's see now," gruffed the mayor. "A walking race . . . hec! A custard pie throwing competition . . . messy. Lavender sachets . . ; . . . Lavender WOTsits? A University Challenge quiz . . . not on your nelly! A sweet factory . . . mmm, I must say that's got appeal. Gob-stoppers! I remember those. One gob-stopper in one's mouth lasted a whole lesson – and longer, if one didn't suck too violently. A jumble sale . . . a jolly old jumble sale – boring I suppose – but at least everyone will come. Better choose that one.

"Now, what prize to give . . ." said the mayor to himself, tottering over to his bookcase. "Better make it a cheap one. Something I don't mind parting with. What! Jolly good! Gosh! – is that the time?"

Mr Bodley looked at the winning letter. He went white, then green, then an awful purple.

The witch had won the competition! Was the mayor stupid or something? That was Lady Fox-Custard's idea. Then he remembered his own rule – must be written down. Her Ladyship would be livid with him. Perhaps if he invited her on to the stage to hand out the prize, that would make it all right. Lady Fox-Custard liked being on the stage. He rang her up.

"Of *course* I don't mind not winning the competition," treacled Lady Fox-Custard, nearly kicking the table from under her Crown Derby pot, "and I shall be

31

delighted to hand over the prize to a dear little child.''

Mr Bodley was about to say that it was the witch and not a little child who had won, but he had used up all his courage for one day.

The children were called into the hall and the prize winner announced. Simon clapped loudly, even though he did know that the jumble sale was his mother's idea, pinched by Lady Fox-Custard, and pinched again by the witch.

Lady Fox-Custard knew also that she had pinched the idea and then had had it pinched from her again by the witch. There was not a lot she could say except, ''I am absolooootely delighted, my good woman, to give you this prize. I do hope you will use it well.''

The witch, who had been expecting something bigger, like a Rolls Royce, or at least a bicycle, flopped a dusty curtsey and stuffed the smallish parcel into her handbag to be opened when she got home.

When at last the bell rang, the witch dashed home the short way round, that is to say, over the fields and through people's back gardens, and straight through Lady Fox-Custard's goldfish pond. She tore open the parcel excitedly, only to find it contained a horrid boring-looking book called *A Thousand And One Things Every Child Should Know*.

''Gosh!'' she exclaimed. ''That's not a prize – it's a blooming punishment.''

Disgusted, she shoved the book under the broken

leg of the television.

The next day, the children were eager to know what the witch had won.

"It was amazing! I got a thousand and one things," she said, not explaining that this was just half the title of a ghastly book.

"You lucky thing!" gasped Jimmy Watson. "Can we come and see some of them?"

"Some of what?" asked the witch.

"Some of the thousand and one things."

"Oh, them," said the witch, "I'm out most nights. I've joined a ballet dancing evening class."

"Oh super!" said Sharon Dupont, "it might be the same one I'm in."

"Mine's in the north of Scotland," lied the witch. Sharon was looking puzzled and the witch was saved by the arrival of Lady Fox-Custard, leading a small, very clean looking boy. She scuttled him up to Miss Phoeble.

"This is my nephew, Cuthbert," she said. "His parents, the Duke and Duchess of Doonuthin are in Africa, on safari. He's a genius you know. I hope you know how to cope with terribly clever children."

Miss Phoeble looked very alarmed, and so too did Sally. Cuthbert sat down and glanced around him.

"Right. Well then," said Miss Phoeble, trying to think of something clever to say next. "As we are going to have a jumble sale soon, the reading lesson will now be changed to a craft lesson." (The witch pretended to look sorry.) "There are plenty of things in the cupboard, but do try to make objects people will want to buy."

The witch dashed to help. She gave out great mounds of messy things, slamming the paper down in crumpled heaps and sloshing glue everywhere. "Try. Try *really hard*!" she said to the children.

"Calm down!" laughed Simon.

"Or better still, go home," snorted Sally.

"More glue?" said the witch, pouring an extra helping on to Sally's desk.

"I'm going to crayon some lovely little pictures and paste them on to match boxes," said Sharon Dupont.

"What for?" asked Jimmy Watson.

Sharon burst into tears.

"I don't know what I said!?" exclaimed Jimmy Watson, startled. Girls never ceased to bewilder him.

Cuthbert smoothed out his bit of paper and looked blank. He had never taken part in a messy lesson before.

Simon started to make a giraffe. To his surprise, the giraffe began to take shape far more easily than he had expected.

"Gosh!" gasped Jimmy, "that's dead good, Simon. How did you get it to look so lifelike?"

"I don't know," Simon said, "I just must be good at making giraffes, and I didn't know I was. Maybe I could do them as a job?"

The other children crowded round, admiringly. "Isn't it great!" they said.

Sally ignored them all. She had gone to a great deal of trouble to design a pyjama case and nobody was looking at it. Not even Miss Phoeble, who liked neat things. But Miss Phoeble too was making a stupid fuss about Simon's giraffe. She had some very special paint which she got out for Simon to use.

"I might even buy this for my mum, if it's not too expensive," said Simon.

"I shouldn't think it will be," said Sally spitefully.

By this time, the witch looked like a litter bin.

"This glue's terribly strong," she was saying, trying to wrench a whole roll of black paper off one side of her face. And as fast as she pulled cotton wool off one hand, it stuck to the other.

"And what are *you* making, dear?" asked Miss Phoeble.

"Would you believe a mess?" snorted the witch.

All this time, Cuthbert had still done nothing, except to continue to be polite. Simon and the boys wondered if he was going to be a dead loss.

It was time to go home, and Simon carefully put his giraffe inside his desk. He had painted it bright green on the back and yellow under its tummy. He could think of nothing else as he raced home. "I've made an absolutely *fantastic* giraffe!" he told his mother as he burst into the kitchen.

"Lady Fox-Custard has just been on the phone," said his mother. "She asked me to make some little fairy cakes for the jumble sale. I can't decide whether to make them chocolate or vanilla."

Back at school, Sally had still not packed up her things. The cleaning lady was coming round the classrooms, sweeping up the mess. Sally's pyjama case was going all wrong. It jolly well wasn't fair. She opened Simon's desk and looked at the giraffe. It glistened, wetly, in the light. Crossly, Sally flung it on the floor and stamped on it.

At home, Simon was still prattling on excitedly to his mother about the giraffe.

"It's funny how I didn't know how easy it was to make them," he was saying.

He was interrupted by the phone ringing. It was the witch.

"You haven't seen my cat anywhere, have you?" she wanted to know.

"No," said Simon.

"Not to worry," said the witch, putting on her hat and coat.

And she went off to the toy shop.

The toy shop had rubber ducks, tigers with plastic

pop eyes, felt frogs, bored looking teddy bears, and mice with keys in them. There was only one cat. It was badly stuffed, made of nylon, and it was ginger.

"How much?" asked the witch.

"Fifteen pounds," said the girl behind the till.

"But it's *ginger*!" exclaimed the witch.

"Fifteen pence," decided the girl, nervously.

"That's more like it — selling cats the wrong colour!" snorted the witch.

She took the cat home and combed it with a toothbrush, dipped in black ink. The cat's fur clogged together, giving it quite a reasonable look of George. The witch had only just arranged the toy cat on the hearthrug when Simon arrived.

"George is back!" was the first thing Simon said.

"Mmm," the witch mumbled.

"He looks tired," said Simon.

38

"He is," agreed the witch, hastily. "He'll stay like that for ages. Weeks maybe. Just ignore him."

Simon couldn't help staring at the cat a bit longer. There was something peculiar about it. But then George was a very peculiar cat. "I just came to remind you that it's the jumble sale on Saturday afternoon you know," he said. "We've got all tomorrow to finish things off. I've only got to paint the spots on my giraffe, and it's finished. What are you doing?"

"I've got a great idea," grinned the witch, "but I'm not telling anyone. Great ideas get stolen."

Simon opened his mouth and shut it again. He stared at George. "Bring him to school tomorrow," he said. "I keep telling everyone about George but they won't believe me."

"Shan't," said the witch.

"Why won't you?"

"Just once then," the witch agreed, huffily.

Next day, she stuffed the toy cat into her handbag so that only the top of his head was showing. She wasn't having anyone saying she was a witch without a cat. As she approached the classroom door, there was a terrible noise.

Everyone was shouting, especially Simon.

"Just *look* what someone's done!" he was yelling.

Underneath his desk lay the remains of his giraffe. It was completely flattened and unmendable.

"It can't have just fallen – someone's *stamped* on it!

Why would anybody want to do that?"

"Somebody dead jealous," said Jimmy Watson.

A few children glanced at Cuthbert, but quickly decided he looked too well behaved.

Miss Phoeble dashed in, wondering what the riot was about. She was shocked when she saw the giraffe.

"It must have been someone terribly mean!" she said. She told Simon that he could have some clay to take home with him, and also, the very special paint.

"I expect I'll be able to make another one," Simon said to Jimmy Watson, as they settled down.

"I think I can see a pussy cat!" piped up Sharon Dupont.

"Not in here, dear," said Miss Phoeble.

"I can, though," said Sharon. "It's sticking out of that old lady's handbag."

"I can see it too!" squeaked Jimmy Watson. "It's glaring, hideously."

"Don't touch him!" warned the witch.

"I'm sorry, dear," started Miss Phoeble, "but animals are not allowed in school. You'll have to . . ."

But the children had started to crowd round the witch's desk.

"Let his nose out." shrilled Sharon Dupont. "He'll smothercate like that."

"He looks dead already to me," said somebody.

"Course he's not dead," spat the witch, "he's just ill. That's why I've brought him with me. He's got molecular molugular."

"Take him home at once then!" gasped Miss Phoeble. "That's sure to be catching!"

Sally was by now leaning right over the witch's desk. She had her suspicions. "That cat doesn't look r...", she started to say, when it was Jimmy Watson's turn to gasp.

"Look at Sally's shoes!" he shouted. "They're covered in giraffe paint!"

The terrible truth dawned on everybody. Sally's face went bright red. She could think of no excuse. Miss Phoeble took her into a corner and a lot of whispering went on. Even the witch could not hear what they were saying. In the end, Sally came up to Simon and said she was sorry.

At Horty Hall that evening, Lady Fox-Custard was asking Cuthbert how he was getting on.

Cuthbert looked excited, "There was a smashing giraffe in school yesterday. It had a ginormous neck until somebody stamped on it, and then there was nearly a riot. Then there was this very old woman who had a cat in her handbag. Someone thought she was trying to smother it, but she wasn't, she was just trying to keep its body temperature stable because it had contracted molecular molugular."

"Good Lor'!" exclaimed Lady Fox-Custard, who couldn't understand one word Cuthbert was saying. "Didn't they teach you no reading and 'rithmetic?"

Miss Phoeble in Love

SIMON sat at the kitchen table, re-making his giraffe, and Jimmy sat next to him, holding the special pots of paint steady.

"It's going to be just as good as the other one," said Jimmy, comfortingly.

The kitchen was full of friendly warm smells as Simon's mother took out tray after tray of fairy cakes from the oven. When they were cool, the two boys helped to ice them and pack them into boxes, ready for the jumble sale. It annoyed Simon a little that his mother should be working so hard when he was pretty sure that Lady Fox-Custard was doing nothing. As it happened, Lady Fox-Custard was doing practically nothing. She needed to rest so that she would look her best the next day. It was up to her, she told Cuthbert, to give the lead to the other ladies in the village, when it came to looking wonderful.

"Can I go out and play?" asked Cuthbert.

"I think not, darling," drawled Lady Fox-Custard. "It looks like rain. Go and help Poppet with the tables for tomorrow. I'll do the flowers when I'm feeling a little stronger."

"Gosh!" thought Cuthbert, as he trudged off in search of Poppet, his aunt looked strong enough to him; as strong as a lion, or an elephant even.

It actually wasn't raining at all and Simon had promised to take Jimmy round to see the witch's house.

"It's only ordinary, really," Simon was saying as they scrunched through the drifts of autumn leaves by the roadside. "It hasn't got a crooked roof or a toadstool for a chimney."

"But I bet it's dead scarey *inside*," shivered Jimmy, hopefully.

The witch didn't hear the boys come in. She was peering at herself in the mirror and trying out different pieces of coloured material round her head.

"Nah," she said. "Nah, nah, maybe. Aha!"

She had blacked out one tooth and darkened her face with gravy browning.

"Eeeeeh!" she screamed, as she turned round and saw the two boys staring at her. "You perishin' little varmints! You could give an old lady a heart attack! What the hec are you doin' creepin' up on me like that?"

"Jimmy wanted to see what your house was like,"

explained Simon.

"Well he's seen it now. He can push off," said the witch, ungraciously.

"Can't I just stroke your cat?" asked Jimmy.

"NO!" shrieked the witch, alarmed. "He's just sitting there waiting for an ambulance. Don't you dare go near him!"

She swooped up the stuffed cat and stuck it violently on the bookshelf.

"Ouch!" winced Jimmy Watson, who could feel the pain George must be feeling. "Look! Underneath his ears has gone a funny gingery colour!"

"Oh dear me!" gasped the witch. "I think you'd

better go home at once; this is more serious than I thought. There could easily be a molugular EPIDEMIC!''

When both boys had gone, the witch threw the toy cat in the dustbin. It was turning out to be a lot more trouble than it was worth. She carried on with her preparations for the jumble sale. In the back of the saucepan cupboard was a cracked goldfish bowl. With her gypsy head dress, dark face, and crystal ball, she would look like a real fortune teller. Oh boy! Would she sock it to them or wouldn't she!

It was sunny the next day. Lady Fox-Custard spent the morning getting ready. She was wearing a dress covered in poppies and cornflowers. The mayor had overslept and was frantically polishing his chain. The witch was worrying about the lasting properties of her gravy browning make-up and Mr Bodley was dreading the whole thing.

At the door of Horty Hall stood Sally. She had forgotten all about the disgrace of standing on Simon's giraffe and was meanly arresting children who were getting into the jumble sale without paying.

''Tickets are ten pence,'' she was saying.

''Fancy having to pay, just to get in, when we've done all the work!'' gasped Jimmy Watson.

''What – like all the gob-stoppers you didn't make in your fantastic sweet factory,'' scoffed Sally.

The witch arrived in a flummox.

"I'm the fortune teller," she said, scattering quite a lot of Sally's ten pence tickets.

Sally did not recognize the witch. Nor did Lady Fox-Custard, who remarked, "That's funny, I don't remember hiring a fortune teller."

The witch made her way to a darkish corner and partly hid herself behind a curtain. She had a notice ready, which said,

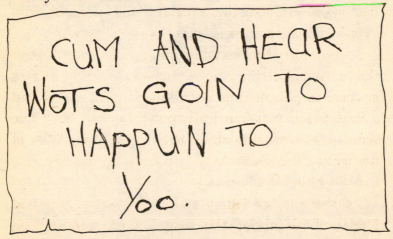

CUM AND HEAR
WOTS GOIN TO
HAPPUN TO
YOO.

At once, a small queue formed as parents and children trooped eagerly towards her. Everybody wanted to know what was going to happen to them. By the time the witch had told them, most of them wished they hadn't. Miss Phoeble, who was marooned on the knitted woollies stall, was dying to have her fortune told. At length she got Sharon Dupont to take over the stall for a little while.

The witch polished up her crystal ball with her sleeve and exclaimed, "Good heavens! This is interesting!"

Miss Phoeble blinked.

"Know any tall dark men?"

Miss Phoeble blinked again.

"Well, tall, dark, and a bit baldy in the middle," corrected the witch.

Miss Phoeble immediately conjured up a picture of her headmaster, Mr Bodley.

"He's madly in love with you," said the witch.

Miss Phoeble wobbled back to her woollies stall. This was something she had never imagined, Mr Bodley – madly in love with her! She sold a pair of bootees for two pence instead of fifty.

The jumble sale was going very well. Simon's mother had sold all her fairy cakes in the first twenty minutes and was in the middle of helping Lady Fox-Custard.

"I just can't think where that fortune teller has come from," Lady Fox-Custard kept saying.

"But she seems awfully good," said Simon's mother. "She's bringing in a lot of money."

Simon had spent his pocket money buying his own giraffe. He was going to hide it until Christmas and then give it to his mother.

The rest of the children were spending their money on ice cream and sausage rolls.

"I don't think this sausage roll would have the strength to roll anywhere," Jimmy Watson was declaring. "It's got about half an inch of sausage in it."

"And that looks dead," sympathized Sharon Dupont.

"I should jolly well hope it is!" said Jimmy.

"Oh my goodness!" the witch was exclaiming for the umpteenth time that afternoon, "and what is this I see in my crystal ball?" In fact, all she could actually see was her own reflection. (She now had Mr Bodley sitting in front of her.) "I see a sad looking lady. She is rather a twittery sort of lady, a teacher I think."

Mr Bodley looked disappointed.

"Ah, yes," the witch went on. "I think it is someone you know. Her name begins with 'F'," said the witch (who didn't know how to spell 'Phoeble'). "She is madly in love with you and you should marry her and take her far far away. The further the better."

Mr Bodley was getting very annoyed. "You're talking a load of nonsense, woman!" he exploded. "It's a waste of ten pence just to hear that!"

"Twenty," cackled the witch.

A lot of the parents were drifting off. They had had a go in the lucky dip, bought some raffle tickets for prizes they hoped they wouldn't win, and had stocked up for the weekend with very nice looking fairy cakes. The mayor too was itching to make his escape. On his way to the door, he caught sight of Lady Fox-Custard's Crown Derby pot on its fancy little table.

"By jove!" he choked. "That's a mighty fine looking pot. How much is it, little boy?" he asked Jimmy Watson, who happened to be standing next to it.

"Five pence," decided Jimmy, pleased at last to be in charge of something.

"I'll take it," said the mayor.

And he left in great haste.

Mr Bodley was in the drawing room, adding up.

"Not bad," he said, "but we still don't have enough money for the old people's home."

"There's still the end of term pantomime, Headmaster," put in Simon's mother.

Yes, indeed," groaned Mr Bodley.

He was interrupted by terrible screams. Surely someone was getting murdered – just as he was off home for his tea.

Poppet was dragging Lady Fox-Custard to a chair. She was in the middle of fainting.

"She's lost her pot," he explained, wafting a bottle of rent-a-butler smelling salts, economy size under her nose.

"I can see that!" exclaimed Mr Bodley.

"Me Crown Derby pot!" wailed Lady Fox-Custard.

"It's missing! I forked out a fortune for that wretched ugly thing and somebody's pinched it!"

Everyone was aghast.

"But if you thought it was so ugly, I don't know why you mind so much," put in Simon's mother.

Lady Fox-Custard stopped fainting long enough to say, "Don't be so stupid!"

On the way home, Simon said, "I don't know why you bother helping that woman when she's so rude to you."

But his mother didn't seem to hear; her cakes had been a success and they were a step nearer reaching their target for the old people's home.

"Pssst!" said Jimmy Watson from the shadows of a shop doorway.

Simon lagged behind.

"What?" he asked.

"It was *me* who sold that awful pot. I sold it to the mayor for five pence. I thought it was meant to be in the jumble sale."

Never had Jimmy Watson looked quite so tragic. Simon looked at him in horror, and then both boys burst out laughing. They rolled around in the ditch, hysterically.

"Come on, you two," called Simon's mother. "I kept a few chocolate cakes back for our tea."

The Big Cheat

ON MONDAY morning Miss Phoeble arrived in a pink mini dress and a bow in her hair. The children gasped, but Miss Phoeble had eyes only for the headmaster. If only she'd known years ago that Mr Bodley was madly in love with her. She shot him a melting look. Mr Bodley was horrified. One of his teachers had gone mad! It would be his turn next. Wherever he went, there was Miss Phoeble, smiling at him, horrifically.

The witch was vastly amused. Lessons seemed to have been forgotten. She scribbled a note and nudged Simon.

"Pass this round," she hissed.

The note said,

MISS FEEBLE IS DIPLY IN LUV WITH MISTAH
BODLEE
AND HE IS DIPLY IN LUV WITH HUR.

Simon giggled, refolded the note and passed it to Jimmy. Jimmy giggled too and passed it to Cuthbert. Cuthbert thought it was terribly funny, but misguidedly passed it to Sally.

"How stupid!" scoffed Sally, loudly.

"I'll take that," Mr Bodley interrupted, swooping like an eagle. "You know what I think about wasting time in school."

He read the note and began to shake in a frightening sort of way. It reminded Jimmy Watson of a film he'd once seen of a volcano just before it erupted.

Suddenly Mr Bodley knew who the fortune teller

had been. He would have to do something about that meddling old hag. He rang the mayor, but the mayor, who thought the witch was a jolly good sort, just said, "I'm sure she was only having a bit of fun, old chap. No one would seriously think anybody could have fallen in love with you – especially that dear little Phoeble person. She seems so sensible."

Mr Bodley would have said something rude, except that the mayor was somebody important.

That evening, he called round to see Lady Fox-Custard. *She* at least was not one of the witch's fans. Lady Fox-Custard was wearing her tiara and playing a game of patience. Cuthbert, much against her wishes, was reading a comic that Poppet had leant him. Poppet took Mr Bodley's hat and umbrella and ushered him into the drawing room.

"And to what do I owe this visit?" treacled Lady Fox-Custard.

"I need advice," grumbled Mr Bodley. "I'm having a spot of bother at school."

"Ah," said Lady Fox-Custard, "Cuthbert did mention there were a great many art and craft and physical education lessons, and not a lot of work being done."

"No, not that . . . did he *really*?" He gave Cuthbert a less than warm glance, ". . . I mean, with that over-mature student I've got in my school. That green-eyed, tatty haired, soup stained old baggage."

"Ah! I think I know who you mean." Lady Fox-Custard narrowed her eyes. "If we speak of the same person — she squashed me begonias."

"Did she really!?" gasped Mr Bodley, who wouldn't have known a begonia from a plate of fish fingers. "You must have been savage! Anyway, what do you think I should do?"

Lady Fox-Custard, who adored having her advice sought, said, "That's simple. Just expel her. You'll need a bit of an excuse of course, but I'm sure she does something awful nearly every day."

"She certainly does," agreed Mr Bodley. "For one thing, she's usually late for school. I'll be waiting for her!"

All this time, Cuthbert had had his ears wide open. He liked the witch very much and was shocked by his aunt's mean suggestion.

"I'm just going to feed the goldfish," he said.

"All right, luvvy duck," agreed Lady Fox-Custard.

Cuthbert did not know where the witch lived, but being clever, he found her address in the phone book.

The witch was surprised to see him — perhaps he was really a spy, or a junior tax inspector, but when Cuthbert had told her all that he had overheard of the plot to expel her, she said, "You're quite a decent sort of sausage! Ta very much."

At the crack of dawn, the witch staggered along the road to school. She kept colliding with hedges and traffic lights because her eyes wouldn't keep open properly.

"Zzzzzz," she could hear herself going, in the middle of a zebra, because she was tired and it was still only half past five in the morning. In her handbag was a flask of tea, a bacon and fried bread sandwich, and some crusty toasted cockroaches. At the school gates, the witch had to wait a further half an hour for the school caretaker to arrive.

"Where the hec have *you* been!?" asked the witch.

"I go to bed during the night time," groused the caretaker.

Mr Bodley too had set his alarm clock early. He

charged his car through the school gates at a quarter to nine. To his amazement, there was the witch, sitting at her desk and finishing her breakfast.

"What are *you* doing here this early!?" he boomed.

"Nothing much really," said the witch. "I've sharpened all the pencils, and done this and that, and a bit of the other. I was really just waiting for the sums lesson to begin. But everyone seems to be coming to school so late this morning."

Mr Bodley was speechless and huffed off, and the witch chuckled to herself and made all the pencils blunt again.

Cuthbert told Simon and Jimmy Watson what his aunt and the headmaster had been up to, and the boys agreed that Cuthbert was a really worthy type and could join their gang.

Cuthbert was pleased and Simon was pleased and Jimmy Watson was pleased, but Mr Bodley was not! He came into the classroom right on hometime and he said, "There will be a school Hallowe'en party next week, but before any of you start dancing around and making merry, we are having EXAMS."

The witch followed Simon home. "Hullo, Mrs Woman," she greeted his mother, "I thought I'd have my tea here."

"Of course, dear," Simon's mother said, wondering what on earth the old lady would like.

"I eat anything," said the witch, helpfully, eyeing

a fly which was wandering up the window. "In school tomorrow we're having eggs and ham, aren't we, Simon?"

Simon racked his brains, and then he burst out laughing. "Mr Bodley said we were going to have EXAMS! Not eggs and ham."

"Never heard of them," the witch sulked.

"Exams are questions and we have to answer them," Simon explained.

"What a cheek!" gasped the witch. "Teachers are getting paid millions of pounds a week and they have to come and ask *us* for the answers."

"Ah, what a shame," said Simon's mother, who could see that the witch didn't understand. "I'm sure you're too old to bother. I wouldn't do the exams, dear."

"Got to," said the witch darkly, "or Mr Bodley will expel me."

"Surely not!" gasped Simon's mother, and gave the witch an extra helping of spaghetti. The witch was a little surprised that Simon would never eat spiders and beetles when he was at her house, yet thought nothing of eating ten foot long orangey coloured worms in his own. But she gobbled up the spaghetti hungrily, wiped her mouth politely on the hem of her skirt and hurried off, saying that she had to go to bed early to be ready for the exam in the morning.

Mr Bodley had been up half the night, searching for

a question that he was sure the witch wouldn't be able to answer. He eventually found one.

"The dreaded question number seven!" he tittered, as he drove along to school, singing,

> "Oh, what a beautiful morning,
> Oh, what a day for a joke,
> I've got a question on learning
> That'll make that old witch woman choke."

The children were waiting, glumly.

"I've got me pencil sharpened," whispered the witch, smugly.

"Ssh," warned Simon, "no talking during exams."

"Of course not," whispered the witch back. "It's just that I feel so excited. I wish we could begin."

Miss Phoeble entered. She had given up wearing her pink mini and she had given up hope, too.

"Give out the papers, Sally," she said. Secretly she thought,

> "Oh what a miserable morning,
> When will I ever get wed?
> I've got a face like a fish cake,
> And my heart is as heavy as lead."

Mr Bodley came in and scowled at everybody, but especially at the witch. If she couldn't answer all the questions, he would expel her! "The exam starts . . . NOW!" he bellowed, and went back to his room.

Everyone started to scribble and sigh. And to sigh and scribble. The witch was finding the exam quite easy. Out of the corner of one eye, she could read Sally's answers. She copied down, '99', 'the dead sea', 'soup', 'George Harrison', 'Woolagong', 'treacle and ginger'. But what was up? Sally was looking gormless. She had reached the dreaded question number seven and couldn't answer it. It said, "How many fleas are there on Omar Papah's favourite camel?"

"I should know that," mumbled the witch, chewing her pencil, "I just can't think."

Neither could anyone else.

"Excuse me, Miss Phoeble," said the witch, squinting viciously. "May I leave the room?"

"No, I'm afraid not," said Miss Phoeble. "You heard what Mr Bodley said."

"Yes, I know," said the witch, "but I *must*. I've just remembered I've left my frying pan on. It will go on fire and all the fat will swoosh over the top and drop on my cat and stick to his fur and burn him to death. And then it will burn across the carpet and up the curtains and through the ceiling into my bedroom, and the bed'll go on fire. And then . . ."

Miss Phoeble by this time was looking very alarmed.

"Oh all right then," she said.

The witch charged off.

Back at home, she grabbed the book, *A Thousand And One Things Every Child Should Know* from under the television leg and stuffed it into her handbag. Perhaps it wasn't such a boring old book after all. Then she made herself a coffee, watched half an hour or so of television, before going back to school.

"Was it all right, dear?" asked Miss Phoeble.

"Was what all right?" said the witch.

"Your frying pan, and the cat?"

"Oh that – yes, I was dead lucky, the firemen got there just in time and they rescued George who was only a bit singed, and I took him to the vet, and the vet said he'd be all right when he'd had a bit of a rest and

something to eat, like a few fish and some cream."

The witch sat down and looked around, slyly. Then she gave an enormous sneeze, opened her handbag, and, pretending to look for a handkerchief, she sneaked an eye through her book. "There are two million and seven fleas on Omar Papah's favourite camel," she read.

"Fancy that!" gasped the witch, "I wonder what flea soup would be like?" She wrote down the answer gleefully. She continued to sneeze, open her handbag, and copy down all the answers.

Sally was deeply suspicious, but was unable to see what the witch was up to. The bell rang.

"Time's up, children," said Miss Phoeble.

"Gosh! I enjoyed that," said the witch, stretching.

"I wonder if I'll come top?"

"What! You! Top!" scoffed Sally, as she collected the papers for Mr Bodley. "You're just an ignorant old rat-bag."

Jimmy waited in terror to see if Sally would be struck dead, but the witch had a secret kind of smile on her face and appeared not to be listening.

When she and Simon arrived home, the first thing Simon noticed was that the newsreader was slipping at great speed to one side of the television.

"Sit still, you fool!" the witch said to him, thumping the book, *A Thousand And One Things Every Child Should Know* back under the television leg.

"Aaaah!" gasped Simon. "Now I understand. You had that book in your handbag all the time! You rotten cheat!"

"Well," pouted the witch, "I did win the lousy book. Wasn't I supposed to use it?"

Then Simon burst out laughing.

"Crumbs!" said the witch. "For a moment then, I thought you'd gone all fusty musty."

And she flattened herself on the hearthrug and cackled herself dizzy.

Witch Hallowe'en Party is Best?

THE WITCH had come top in the exam. Mr Bodley would not have told her, but Miss Phoeble had let it out.

"That teacher really was . . . really was . . . *feeble*!" thought Mr Bodley.

"Didn't I do well?" hooted the witch, booming round the classroom like a crazed kangaroo.

She stopped at Sally's desk and leant against it heavily. "I said, didn't I do well? I came *top*, you know."

"I don't know how you did it," muttered Sally, "but . . ."

"But what?" said the witch, looking dangerous.

"Sit down, dear," pleaded Miss Phoeble, "and let's all just get on with a lovely art lesson about Hallowe'en. There's plenty of black paper, and milk straws for witches' broomsticks, and cotton wool for making hair. The best pictures can go round the hall wall for the Hallowe'en dance.''

The children went quiet with contentment. All of them loved cutting out, and pasting things down. Even Cuthbert had got used to making a mess. Sharon Dupont was cutting out the tiniest witches imaginable.

''They look a bit like fairies,'' Jimmy Watson started to say – when he saw Sharon's face starting to crumple up, yet again, and added hastily, ''but only a little bit, they mostly look like fierce and absolutely terrifying witches.''

He wiped his forehead with his sleeve.

''Thank you, Jimmy,'' said Sharon, ''I wanted them to look terrifying.''

''I can't draw witches!'' complained the witch, throwing another lump of paper on the floor.

"Just go and look in the loo mirror!" sniggered Sally.

The witch started to lurch towards Sally, when the bell rang.

"Finish off your things at home," squeaked Miss Phoeble.

Simon and Jimmy Watson sat at the kitchen table. They were feeling excited because Simon's mother had given each of them a pumpkin.

"You won't believe it," Simon's mother was saying, "but they were just lying on the garden path. The milk had disappeared, but those pumpkins were there."

The boys were going to make them into Hallowe'en lanterns. Oddly, somebody had already started to cut away the insides. It would be easy to cut out noses and eyes and fix a candle in the hollow to make a lantern.

"Another thing," Simon's mother went on, "my washing was all over the ground, and your bike was knocked over too. It seems strange. It's not as if it was windy."

"Sounds spooky!" shivered Jimmy, pleasantly. "I always think the sky looks all different near Hallowe'en."

"How's that, dear?" said Simon's mother.

"I don't know, really, it looks bigger and draughtier, and emptier − as if it was waiting for something to happen in it. Like funny moons popping up, or bats dashing about, or witches screaming across it."

"You're as bad as Simon!" laughed Simon's mother.

There was a swooshing noise outside the kitchen door, and then a flump, followed by some bad tempered muttering. The witch knocked and walked straight in, propping her broomstick against the wall.

"Could I borrow a shovel, Mrs Woman?" she asked. "There's a whole load of soot just come down my chimney. Flup, it went, just everywhere, and I'd only just finished dusting."

Simon choked. The witch had never dusted anything in her whole life.

"You poor thing," said Simon's mother, handing the witch a shovel. "You do seem to have a lot to put up with lately. Shouldn't you be able to get a home help at your age?"

"Mmmm, but they *disturb* things," grunted the witch. "I like to know where I've put stuff."

"Of course," agreed Simon's mother.

She told the boys they could light their pumpkin lanterns and take the witch home.

The witch's kitchen was indeed knee high in soot, and the boys had to work hard to get it clear.

"Don't you think there's something weird going on?" Simon said.

"Maybe there is, and maybe there isn't," said the witch, looking up the chimney as if she half expected to find something there.

"I just hope there's no more of the rotten stuff to come down, because I'm having a party here on Hallowe'en night."

"But there's a party at school," reminded Jimmy.

"So what," said the witch, "I've *always* had a party at Hallowe'en. I'm expecting my sister, Tombola."

"The one who lives in Africa?" gasped Simon.

"Certainly," said the witch.

There was an enormous crash outside the door.

"That sounds like her now," said the witch. "She's still rotten at landings."

The witch opened the door and poked her nose out. Tombola was lying in the bushes with both legs stuck in the air. Her broomstick had snapped in half and her pet gorilla, Banana, was pulling soil and squashed cabbage out of his fur. Jimmy Watson tried to scream, but no noise would come out of his mouth.

"Hullo, love," greeted Tombola, getting herself the right way up for a conversation and yanking Banana into the house. "I would've landed better than that, but there's a lot of traffic up in the sky tonight. It was perfectly clear when I left Africa, and then, just past Gatwick I ran into all these dark lumps."

"Planes?" said the witch.

"I know a plane when I see one!" snorted Tombola.

"No, Banana thought they were probably UFO's. They affected my steering."

By this time, Banana had recovered from his long flight and was bombing around the kitchen, looking for food. He had also just discovered the stuffed cat in the bin and was tearing it to shreds to see what it was made of. Jimmy was still opening and shutting his mouth. The sky had opened up and delivered a new, highly unusual and terrifying witch; a gorilla who travelled a lot, had sophisticated knowledge of unidentified flying objects, and yet thought nothing of tearing apart a cat which didn't belong to him.

The witch said hastily, "Hadn't you two better be

going?'' She hurried the boys to the door.

"That wasn't the witch's cat," said Simon, as he and Jimmy trailed home. "I wonder where George is?"

Next day, Cuthbert was busy telling everyone about the goings-on at Horty Hall gardens. The goldfish had disappeared from the pond, several trees had had their tops knocked off, and there was a scorch mark on the roof.

"All I could see," said Cuthbert, "was a couple of dark shapes by the tool shed. They looked like terribly old women, but they could have been a couple of black bin liners flapping in the wind."

Mr Bodley whizzed through Assembly, sent the children back to their classrooms, and was about to escape to his office, when two people arrived at the far end of the hall. They were strangers, and both of them were dressed in long black coats.

"Oh no!" muttered Mr Bodley to himself — they must be school inspectors. School inspectors swooped without warning and he was due for a visit. This was something he dreaded daily and now it was happening. School inspectors were both posey and nosey. The two women were, in fact, related to the witch and were called Hatty The Howl and Minnie The Moan. For a night and a day they had been roaming the area, searching for the witch's house. Witches are drawn to one another at Hallowe'en. Hatty and Minnie were completely lost. They were about to ask Mr Bodley if he could direct them to the witch's house, when the peculiar man started shaking hands with them.

"I've been expecting you," Mr Bodley was saying.

"Actually," started Hatty The Howl, "we're lost. We were looking for . . ."

"Not to worry, ladies," interrupted Mr Bodley. "You're here now. I expect you'd like to look round the school."

"School!" Minnie The Moan started to shudder and turn green, and then red, and then yellow, like a set of traffic lights just about to pack in.

"Well, just one classroom then," added Mr Bodley, who wondered why the education office should send him such ancient and wild looking inspectors.

He led the two witches along to Miss Phoeble's classroom and tapped with pretence politeness on the door.

As soon as they entered, Hatty and Minnie recognized the witch.

They were about to hoot hullo to her, when she shot them a warning look and put her finger to her lips. Hatty The Howl winked, and said to Mr Bodley, "I see you take pensioners in this class. That's nice."

"Oh yes indeed!" smarmed Mr Bodley. "This particular old hag . . . old woman, has learning difficulties."

The witch buried her nose in her history book and

began to breathe and read very loudly . . . "King Alfred burnt the cakes, — he must have been a dumbo!"

"Shush, my dear," interrupted Miss Phoeble. "We've got very special visitors."

"Where?" asked the witch, looking under her desk and all about her.

"They've come to see how we work," added Miss Phoeble, trembling like a school dinner jelly.

"Ah!" exclaimed the witch. "I'm so sorry. It's just that I'm not used to proper lessons. You see, we usually have mucking about lessons. I like them best. Mostly, we just cut out, and glue, and paint, and throw bean bags, and have extra playtimes, and do-as-you-like-lessons, and read this and that and draw a picture of it sort of lessons.''

''Please!'' gasped Miss Phoeble. She could see Mr Bodley's face was turning a very strange colour.

The witch hesitated. ''What?'' she said. ''Were you just going to say you were letting us out early again?''

''And you mean, you don't never have *proper* lessons?'' exclaimed Hatty The Howl.

''Only improper,'' said the witch.

There was a knock at the door and a child popped her head round to tell Mr Bodley that there were two school inspectors waiting for him in his office.

''Then who . . .?'' began Mr Bodley.

Minnie and Hatty looked at their watches and said, ''Gosh! Is that the time?'' and vamooshed in a puff of foul-smelling smoke.

Back at the witch's house, there was a great deal of cackly laughter.

''How did you manage that foul smell?'' chortled the witch.

''It's a new recipe of mine, dear heart,'' guffawed Hatty The Howl. ''We had to get out of that boring place somehow.''

''And the trouble we had finding you!'' added Minnie The Moan, '' – off and on roofs, through back gardens . . .''

''and goldfish ponds!'' tittered Hatty.

''I got soaked,'' Minnie moaned on. ''And people

round here leave their washing out in the dark, and I flew straight into a string vest. I thought, Hey up! It's a witch trap!''

"And then she fell headlong over a boy's bike," giggled Hatty.

"And I suppose it was the pair of you scrubbling about round my chimney, and making all that soot come down!" declared the witch.

"And I bet it was them I bumped into over Gatwick!" shrilled Tombola, in her loud, jungle sort of voice.

Banana, loped up from the floor, sniffed all round Minnie and Hatty, raised his nose to the ceiling in a wiffling sort of way and then decided that the foul smell lingering round them was the same smell as the unidentified flying objects they'd bumped into over the airport.

"So!" interrupted Hatty, who could feel an argument brewing, "let's talk about the Hallowe'en party. That's what we've all come for after all. Not to fight and smell each other. *What* are we going to wear and *what* are we going to eat?"

"What am I going to wear?" Lady Fox-Custard was asking Cuthbert, who was reading another of Poppet's comics.

"For what?" he asked, absently.

"The Hallowe'en party of course!" yelled his aunt. "Honestly, Cuthbert, sometimes I think you don't know how h'important we are. It's up to us to look the best."

She rang for Poppet and told him to bring every dress she had in her wardrobe.

"As you wish, Ma'am," bowed Poppet, giving Cuthbert the most enormous nudge as he walked past him.

"Oh I hate these do's," grumbled the mayor. His shirt had just popped another button. He wondered if there'd be boring old quiche again. And boring old flaky pastry do-dahs which always erupted and dodahd down the front of his robes. Nobody ever thought to offer him bacon on fried bread, just these utterly ghastly, inadequate, yukky, designer creations.

Miss Phoeble had found a really super little dress in Oxfam. Simon's mother had an outfit she always wore, and the children were dressed up as tigers, and rabbits, fieldmice, cuddly bears, fairies, ghosts, pterodactyls, and very unsociable looking decimal points. Sally was in a white pussy cat costume.

"Oh, *you* again!" sighed Jimmy Watson, when he found Sally selling tickets at the hall door. "Can't you not go blooming nowhere without flipping paying?"

"I didn't want to come either," said Simon, as he and his friend flopped in a corner to eat their flaky pastry do-dahs. "You know the witch is having a party don't you?"

"I didn't," said Jimmy. "Why aren't we at *it*?"

A terrible green nose of enormous length, slid through the hall window. "Why *aren't* you at my party?" said a voice behind it.

"Because you didn't ask us," said Simon to the witch.

"Silly little twitty boy!" scoffed the witch. "Pass the word round. My friends and relations want someone to dance with. They want someone to play duck-apple with, and, who-can-jump-on-the-pumpkin-hardest with, and hunt-the-bat with, and I-spy-ten-little-spiders with."

"Gosh!" gasped Jimmy, feeling the hairs rise on the back of his neck. "Let's go, Simon!"

The mayor was dancing with Lady Fox-Custard,

when Simon, Jimmy, and most of the children in the class, slithered out of the school hall.

The noise coming from the witch's house was so deafening that even the cabbages in the garden were being rocked in their rows.

"Hec!" whispered Jimmy, "she'll get a police raid."

The witch opened the door to them and the children were nearly flattened by the vibrations of 'I'm in love with you, baby. Swing me, do.'

"Grab a partner!" yelled the witch, dragging them indoors.

To Jimmy's horror, he found himself in the iron clutches of Banana.

"I love to boogie!" Banana gibbered, "I love to bounce my partner on the wall. I love to . . ."

"Put that boy down!" yelled Tombola. "You big . . . big . . . GORILLA!"

Banana had already dropped Jimmy in the waste paper bin because he had just spotted Miss Phoeble entering. She had only called to find out where all her children had got to. She was not expecting to be treated like a human yoyo, or a football at a cup final, or a toy teacher in a game of booma boomas. Tombola hit Banana sharply on his hairy head and stuffed Miss Phoeble under the table for safekeeping.

No one heard the siren on the top of Constable Scuff's police car. One minute he wasn't dancing with Hatty The Howl, and the next minute he was.

"What a gorgeous little man!" Hatty was howling, stuffing Constable Scuff's notebook, unwritten on, back into his pocket. Constable Scuff eyed the refreshments, which looked delicious, and decided he was probably off duty anyway.

Back at the school hall, Sally was about the only child left. The mayor was muttering about having to be up for a meeting in the morning and escaped into the road. Outside, he could hear the strains of loud music in the distance. He sighed. *Someone* was having a jolly Hallowe'en party.

"I'll just drive home nice and slowly," he said to himself, "who knows, there might be some *real* witches not so many miles away, and some *real* magic."

The Very Sleepy Beauty

IT WAS snowing heavily, and that made Simon feel unbearably excited.

"I'm grounded!" grumbled the witch, flinging her broomstick back into a corner.

"You couldn't fly in this weather anyway," said Simon. "It's getting terrifically thick. Doesn't it make you feel Christmassy?"

"No," said the witch. "Pass me gum boots."

But Simon could tell the witch was a little bit excited by the way she behaved all the way to school. She was like a dog, running round in huge circles. By the time the school bell went, most of the children were soaking wet and the radiator was soon smothered in scarves and gloves. The witch's gloves still had two full sized snowballs in them, which melted quickly and trickled across the room and out of the door. The witch watched the small river with fascination and had only just time to make a paper boat and launch it on its way when Miss Phoeble came in.

"We didn't do terribly well from the Hallowe'en party," she said. "The door money was quite good, but the refreshments weren't sold."

"Musta been a better party somewhere else," said the witch.

Miss Phoeble stared for a moment, vaguely unsure, but added, "Yes, perhaps there was, dear, but let's get on with the pantomime arrangements."

"Cinderella!" cried Sally.

"We had that last year, dear. Don't you remember, you were Cinderella? I thought we'd do the Sleeping Beauty," Miss Phoeble went on, "and I thought we'd do the casting this morning."

"The wotsing?" hissed the witch.

"Casting," Simon told her. "That means choosing who's going to play what."

"Ah," said the witch. "I think I'll choose to play the Sleeping Beauty."

Jimmy fell off his chair, laughing inside the neck of his jumper.

"I'll do the sleeping girl for you, Miss," she said.

"Ah, well . . ." began Miss Phoeble, looking round for help.

"*She'd* be no good, Miss," interrupted Sally. "Look at her! I'll do it, shall I?"

"Well, yes, . ." Miss Phoeble started.

"Why should *SHE*!" yelled the witch. "I've got long hair, same as her. I can put lipstick on, and that eye thingummy stuff, and I can lie down and go to sleep. *Any* dumb cluck can do that!"

She got up, threw herself at Miss Phoeble's feet and shut her eyes. In seconds, the witch was fast asleep. Her chest heaved up and down like a huge pair of bellows, making the toast crumbs on her cardigan shudder and wobble. Her feet stuck up into the air like a pair of life boats, and a small whistling noise, coming from her mouth, fluttered a lump of grey hair which had fallen across her nose.

"Gosh!" said Jimmy in an awed whisper. "She looks like a sunken ship!"

"Revolting!" exclaimed Sally. "She looks more like

a sleeping disaster!''

This uncalled for remark roused the witch from her slumbers and she sat up, refreshed, and ready for more words with Sally.

"I'm the teacher!" shrieked Miss Phoeble, "and I'll choose."

The whole class sat up straight and stared at Miss Phoeble in utter astonishment.

"She's having a nervous breakthrough!" gasped Jimmy, fascinated. Miss Phoeble explained to the witch that the part of the wicked fairy was really a much better part than any of the others. There was more to do and more to say and it was much harder to act than the part of the Sleeping Beauty. The witch looked impressed at this but still not sure. "And as well as having the best part, you can be Sally's understudy," added Miss Phoeble, brilliantly.

"Her underwotsit!?"

"Study!" scolded Simon. "She means, if Sally's off sick, or something, you get to play her part for her."

"Oh," said the witch.

"Can I be the good little fairy then?" piped up Sharon Dupont.

"D'you mean there's a *good* fairy?" asked the witch, indignantly.

"Why can't I . . .?"

"Oh honestly!" said Simon. "You can't be everybody! The good fairy just comes on for two minutes and says something about undoing the wicked fairy's spell and everything'll be all right in the end."

"Oh she does, does she?" muttered the witch.

And Jimmy noticed one of her eyes turn green and roll around on its own. He shivered.

Miss Phoeble continued with the rest of the casting. Jimmy was to be the king; Sarah Grimshaw, the queen; Tim, the chef's cat, and Simon had got the part of the Lord High Chancellor, which was good because there were no words to it. The best male part went to Cuthbert who was to play the prince. Unbeknown to anyone, Lady Fox-Custard had had a word with Mr Bodley about it the night before.

"Poshness is in 'is blood, you see," she had told him. "'E'd be a dead ringer for the prince, h'almost one 'imself. And it'd look a bit funny if I was sitting in the front row, next to the mayor, if Cuthbert was to be seen doing Nobody, you understand?"

Mr Bodley had understood.

"If it goes on snowing like this," gasped Simon, as they went back to the witch's house the long way round, "there won't be any rehearsal tomorrow, because the school'll be fifty feet under the snow!"

"D'you reckon?" said the witch, thoughtfully.

She bashed her way through her snowy cabbages to her front door. "I specially want to hear the weather forecast," she said.

She was just in time to hear the forecaster saying . . . "Heavy winds will cause drifting in some parts and people are asked not to travel unless their journey is really necessary."

The weather forecast was followed immediately by a newsflash. It said, — "News is just reaching us of massive vandalism in the Georgian furniture section of the Victoria and Albert Museum. It is not known yet what is causing the furniture to collapse. The chief curator suspects the damage has, and is being done, either by an army of wood-eating beetles, or by some monster rare species of rat."

The cameras were showing the interior of the museum. Both Simon and the witch were certain they spotted a cat's head, peeping out from under a derelict looking chaise-longue. Its black face was freckled with sawdust and it was looking extremely deceitful.

"Gosh!" exploded Simon. "That was *George!*"

"What was?" mumbled the witch, who had also spotted her long lost cat.

"On the telly!" said Simon. "He was in the Victoria and Albert Museum, eating all their best furniture!"

"Never!" scoffed the witch. "You're seeing things. I think you must be sickening for something. I'm going to end up having to do your part as well if you don't watch out!"

She bustled Simon out of the door before he could say any more.

"So THAT'S where me wretched cat is!" she said to herself. "Well so long as he doesn't give his name and address, or lead any policemen back to me – he can stuff himself with sawdust!"

She sat down to write an important letter. It said,

Dear Salliees Muther.
The Sno is too Dip to get to Scool.
There is drifftun and blowin in finustair
And huffins and puffins in Portland
and Polar Bears on the rampage and
it is too Dainjruss to send yor
Dorter to Scool.
The Hedmastur

The witch checked her letter over for spelling mistakes and was pleased to find there were none. Then she slithered down West Road to Sally's house.

Sally's mother was astonished when she discovered the letter. "This is incredible!" she said.

"It's unreadable you mean!" scoffed Sally, who could recognize the witch's sooty fingerprints.

The witch arrived in school next morning in a rare good mood. "Morning, Bodley," she boomed, shooting her umbrella in and out rapidly to get the snow off it. "Morning, Miss Phoeble. I'm ready to start that underwotsit thingy today."

"It'll be sums first, I expect," said Sally.

The witch shot into the corner to sharpen pencils. After two dozen fierce whizzes at the handle of the pencil sharpener, she emerged with a tin of inch long pencils. Sally stared at them, pointedly, and smiled.

"So that plot hadn't worked," thought the witch. What else kept children off school? Spots! That was it. Teachers were scared of children with spots; especially if they were huge, purple, scabby ones, like the spots she was just going to give Sally now. She wiggled her wand slyly in Sally's direction and watched with glee as the spots began to grow and spread on Sally's face.

"Arrrrgh!" screamed the witch.

"What?" said everybody.

"Look at Sally's face! Aren't those purple things

terribly dangerous and infectious?"

"What things?" cried Sally, alarmed.

"Go and look in the loo mirror," said the witch.

Sally returned, wailing, and was promptly taken home by the care-lady.

"Right," said the witch. "Let's get on."

The children struggled through a rehearsal with the witch doing Sally's part and her own and everybody else's wherever she thought they were flagging.

"Gosh!" complained Jimmy. "Every time I open my mouth to say, 'Send out a proclamation to all my people,' she covers my mouth up with the back of her sleeve and says something different."

"Well, I don't like that bit," complained the witch. "Sending out proclums. What are proclums, for goodness sake? Why can't the king send out something we can all understand — like mint choc ices — anything 'cept blooming proclums?"

Meanwhile, Sally had been sitting in the doctor's surgery for so long, that by the time it came to her turn, the terrible spots had completely vanished. The doctor was very annoyed and told Sally and her mother to go away and stop wasting his time. The witch was annoyed too, but decided that the wicked fairy was a far more interesting part after all and the rest of the term carried on quite peacefully. Miss Phoeble even began to think the pantomime was going to be all right.

"I've found this wonderful suit in the attic," Lady Fox-Custard was saying. "Just look at the lace!"

"I can't wear *that*!" gasped Cuthbert in horror. "My friends wouldn't speak to me."

"Don't be silly!" tutted his aunt. "They'll be jealous, more like it."

Simon and Jimmy were luckier, they were only having to put up with pyjamas and tablecloths.

Mr Bodley shoved his head through the classroom door. "This had better be good," he threatened. "The mayor is coming and he's used to good shows."

Miss Phoeble winced.

It was snowing harder than ever as the parents trudged their way down the school road. The children were crowded into one room behind the stage, giggling, pushing each other and generally wailing for more safety pins. Sally sat to one side, stiff in her Sleeping Beauty outfit and determined not to get it ruined before she went on. The witch too was sitting quietly.

"You look great in that," said Simon, staring uncertainly at the witch's costume.

The witch was wearing a short black ballet dress which stuck out round her hips in rather a threatening sort of way, thick white woollen tights, and on her head was a diamond tiara which was secured under her chin by a quantity of looped elastic.

The curtains opened jerkily and the pantomime began. An incredibly ugly looking doll was the centre of the stage as ten fairies tripped on and off, bestowing their magic christening gifts on her.

"Ten! It was a bit much!" thought the mayor, "and all of them saying, 'and I give you this, and I give you that'."

Then the witch arrived, making Jimmy jump, and shoving the fairies out of the way.

"And I say," she boomed, looking round to see if everyone was looking at her, "that when the princess is twenty-one, she will prick her finger with a needle and DIE!"

A small piece of scenery fell down. "She will die a horrible death. It'll be dead slow. There'll be blood everywhere (Miss Phoeble looked at her script). One minute she'll be alive and kicking, the next minute she'll be stone dead." She stared at the ugly doll as if it was Sally herself and added, "and she'll never be able to act again."

"Oh no!" groaned Simon inside his cloak.

But the mayor was beginning to titter.

Sharon Dupont entered timidly and squeaked, "No, no, she shall *not* die. She shall sleep for a hundred years and a prince will come and wake her up with a kiss."

"Oh yeah?" roared the witch, poking Sharon in the

ribs with her wand. Sharon ran away and the witch beamed at the audience.

"You *ruined* that bit!" barked Sally in the classroom. "You'd better behave yourself in my scene."

"Me!" gasped the witch. "I'm only doing my best acting."

"*You* know what I mean," said Sally.

In the next scene, Sally went up the stairs to the room in the tower where the witch was sitting beside the dreaded spinning wheel. She knocked.

"Gotter now!" whispered the witch to the audience, "Come in."

"Oh, good morning, old woman," acted Sally.

"Old woman! she calls me," confided the witch. "She's going to get killed in a minute you know. Come

over here, my dear, and I'll show you how the needle in this spinning wheel works."

"Spinning wheel?" said Sally.

"She's deaf as well as daft," chortled the witch.

Sally was getting muddled at all the unexpected changes to the script, and angry too. She pricked her finger on the needle and collapsed, carefully, on to the bed. The curtains were hastily pulled across and everybody clapped.

"Gosh! I'm enjoying doing this," chatted the witch, as Miss Phoeble re-pinned most of her costume for her. "I'm dead glad I'm not acting the boring old Sleeping Beauty."

"You're just acting the fool!" fumed Sally. "You spoilt my bit."

"Yes, dear," added Miss Phoeble. "You must try to stick to the story."

"All right." said the witch.

"You'll see my nephew in this next scene," Lady Fox-Custard was telling the mayor.

"Oh really," said the mayor.

"He's wearing an antique satin and lace costume,"

"Oh, really," said the mayor again. Why it was always his misfortune to get dumped next to Lady Fox-Show-Off, he just didn't know.

"That old woman character's good," he remarked to Mr Bodley. "Very promising actress you've got there, Bodley.''

''Mm,'' said Mr Bodley, grimly.

The caretaker yanked the curtains open.

The children were standing like statues, ''asleep''. Some of the silly ones who had chosen to stand on one leg were wobbling a lot. Sally was still asleep where she had fallen, when Cuthbert came hacking his way through the hundred-year hedge.

''Here he comes!'' hooted Lady Fox-Custard.

The hundred-year hedge, which had been made of ordinary thin paper and crayoned by the Infants, had developed the most extraordinary prickles which were tearing Cuthbert's antique suit to ribbons.

''Look what you're *doing*!'' shrieked Lady Fox-Custard.

''What?'' asked Cuthbert, bewildered, and looking down at his horrid suit.

''Who allowed that dangerous hedge in a school play?'' his aunt shrieked on.

The witch, who wasn't in the third scene, was peeping through a gap at the back of the stage. A little more of her appeared.

Cuthbert knelt down by the Sleeping Beauty and was about to kiss her, when a wild looking furry animal sprang from nowhere and settled at Sally's feet. The creature seemed to be blown up to an unusual size and it had, what looked like, the remains of a chair leg in its mouth. Mangled into the fur on its

chest was a sticker which said VICTORIA AND
ALBERT MUSEUM.

"S'George!" gasped the Lord High Chancellor.

"My dumb cat!" exclaimed the witch, who now
had her head and shoulders through the curtain.

"That's an unusual bit," applauded the mayor.
"That cat's one of those animal stars I suppose."

But the witch could see that Constable Scuff, who
was sitting right at the back of the hall, was edging up
and trying to read the sticker. Any minute, she and
her cat would be arrested and thrown into prison for
criminal damage. Hastily she wriggled her wand at
George's chest and the words on the sticker changed
to read – BE KIND TO DUMB ANIMALS. Sally was
trying, quietly, not to scream as the loathsome animal

leant heavily on her foot and started to purr like a motor bike.

Cuthbert kissed her and she tried to wake up but couldn't. He kissed her again, but still Sally couldn't move. The witch was now completely on the stage. She was smiling and peering into the darkness at the audience to see if there was anyone she knew. She cocked her head at Sally – "She's not going to wake up, is she!" she cackled.

The mayor cackled too.

The witch started to do a dance which she'd just made up.

Cuthbert, who was looking consternated, hissed to Miss Phoeble in the wings, "I don't have to kiss her again do I, Miss?"

"Aaah!" laughed all the parents. "Poor little mite!"

"Perhaps she's forgotten what to do," Miss Phoeble hissed back.

"I haven't!" complained Sally. "Something's stopping me moving."

She glared at the witch suspiciously, but the witch was now at the front of the stage reciting fifty verses of a poem she'd just composed. The children standing on one leg at last fell over and were obliged to laugh. This disturbed the cat who leapt off the bed and sniffed round the children to see what was the matter with them. Mr Bodley would have been livid, except that for some reason the mayor seemed to be enjoying himself hugely.

"And now comes the mushy bit," announced the witch. "We gotta have a wedding. Looks as if I'll have to marry the prince. That girl's forgotten her part."

"I haven't" whined Sally. But nobody heard her for the witch was yelling, "Here comes the bride, forty inches wide . . ." And Cuthbert was delighted to get away from Sally and was singing as well.

"Isn't he wonderful!" sighed Lady Fox-Custard.

"That old woman is," said the mayor.

He stood up to clap. "Bravo!" he shouted. "This is the best school pantomime I've ever been to."

"Thank you, Your Mudship," beamed the witch.

The final curtain fell and the caretaker rolled it up and carried it off under his arm, swearing.

"That turned out really great," Simon said to his friend, the witch.

"Of course it did!" the witch said. "Next year, perhaps they'll give me the best part at the beginning instead of messing around making me do boring things first."

She set off at high speed through the snow.

"Where are you going now?" puffed Simon.

"Home," panted the witch, "I've got a whole load of stockings to hang up."

"What on earth for?" Simon asked.

"Christmas, of course," said the witch.